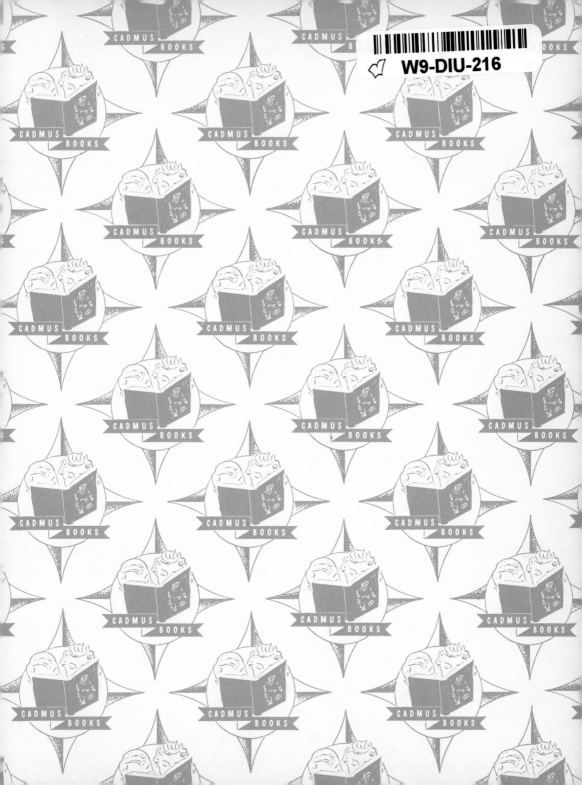

# THE TALE
# THAT GREW
# AND GREW

*by*

## Christiane Grautoff

pictures by

*Anne Marie Jauss*

**1961 First Cadmus Edition**

THIS SPECIAL EDITION IS PUBLISHED BY ARRANGEMENT WITH
THE PUBLISHERS OF THE REGULAR EDITION
STERLING PUBLISHING CO., INC.
BY

# E. M. HALE AND COMPANY
EAU CLAIRE, WISCONSIN

# THE TALE THAT GREW AND GREW

By CHRISTIANE GRAUTOFF
*Pictures by* ANNE MARIE JAUSS

"The crow, she lied about a mouse.
The lie grew bigger than a house,
And from this teeny-weeny bubble
Came plenty, yes plenty, oh, plenty of trouble!"
This is an amusing tale of an eavesdropping crow and the
trouble she caused in the forest among the animals.

**K**

Dewey Decimal Classification: Fic

Library of Congress Catalog Card No. 55-10371

© Copyright, 1955, by
Sterling Publishing Company, Inc.
215 East 37th Street, New York 16, N. Y.

*All Rights Reserved*

Manufactured in the United States of America

It had been a very hot summer. All the animals who lived in the woods were exhausted from the heat. They only left their homes in the morning to do their marketing, and late at night, to rush to the nearest brook to cool themselves. To make matters worse, the animals were bored, for nothing interesting ever happened.

At a little brook, a nice old beaver lived with his wife and daughter, in a beautiful lodge which he had built. Nearby was a willow tree, its low-hanging branches almost touching the beaver's lodge.

In this willow tree a skinny old crow had made her home. She was so very old she could no longer fly. But her eyes and ears were still quite good, so she tried to see and hear everything that went on about her. She was always peeping in the beaver's windows, but because

the green leaves of the tree barred the view,
she could see nothing.

So, during the long, hot summer evenings,
she rocked to and fro and strained her ears to

hear all she could of the beaver family's conversation. And often she would say to herself, "What did he say?" and "Oh, dear, I think I missed something."

On one of the hottest evenings of the summer the beaver sat in front of his lodge, dangling his feet in the water and smoking his pipe. He felt well and happy. His wife and daughter were inside trying to sleep.

While the old beaver sat there smoking his pipe, a little mouse came along hoping to find some relief from the heat. She sat down near the beaver. The beaver's pipe filled the air with smoke, and it seemed to the mouse that the brook water was getting warmer and warmer. Finally the mouse squeaked, "For heaven's sake, Mr. Beaver, stop holding your pipe so close to the water. You're making it so hot, your feet will soon get red!"

The beaver answered, "My dear mouse, my feet are so hot now, the fur seems positively singed."

The skinny old crow stopped rocking and mumbled, "What did he say? I wish I'd heard!" and she strained her ears, not to miss a word.

The little mouse dipped her tail in the water, and quickly withdrew it. "Ugh!" she said, "I almost burned myself! Mr. Beaver, please stop sucking on your pipe! Do you want to cook me?"

The old beaver laughed. "I hardly think you would taste good."

"Oh-h-h," said the little mouse, "don't talk so loud. Someone might hear you! Oh, dear," she sighed, dipping first one foot and then the other in the running water, "the water is so warm the air feels almost cool. I wouldn't be surprised if my feet were quite boiled!"

"Boiled mice feet!" chuckled Mr. Beaver. "What an unattractive thought!"

"How insulting!" cried the mouse. "How can you talk like that!"

The beaver laughed but stopped when the crow suddenly shouted, "What a horrible thing!" and with that, slammed down a branch with such a bang, that the mouse almost fell into the brook, it frightened her so.

"That silly old crow," whispered Mr. Beaver to the mouse. "She was eavesdropping again." After that the two whispered a little longer and then said good night and parted.

The sun wasn't up yet when the crow climbed down from her willow tree. She hopped along the big path which led to the market place.

Once there, she sat down and looked about her, first from left to right, then before and behind her, and then again from right to left. All the time she was muttering: "Wait till I meet someone; wait till I meet someone."

When the first sun rays came out, along
came Mrs. Woodchuck, merrily swinging her
basket. The crow stopped her by waving her
walking stick and cawed, "It's good to meet
you, Mrs. Woodchuck. I can't wait another
minute to tell you . . ."

"What's up? What's up?" said Mrs. Woodchuck.

"Oh, what a terrible thing I saw last night," croaked the crow.

"Tell me quickly," said the woodchuck. So the crow came closer and said, "Well, you won't believe it, but the old beaver threw a mouse into some hot water."

"Oh, what an awful thing to do!" cried Mrs. Woodchuck as she took up her basket.

"Haven't *you* anything to tell me?" asked the crow. But the woodchuck shook her head and ran off, leaving the crow to mutter: "What a pity. What a real pity."

When Mrs. Woodchuck came to the market to buy a carrot from Mrs. Rabbit's stand, she

said, "Have you heard what happened last night?"

"No," said Mrs. Rabbit.

So the woodchuck told her, "Well, a beaver had a fight with a mouse, and threw her into boiling water."

"How dreadful!" cried Mrs. Rabbit.

As she went on with her selling, she thought of the poor mouse that certainly did not deserve so cruel a fate.

Just then, along came Mr. Raccoon. He was hungry and wanted his breakfast. But before he could say a word Mrs. Rabbit cried,

"Have you heard what happened last night?
Mr. Beaver had a fight with a mouse, threw her
into boiling water, and cut her up into several
pieces."

"How terrible!" exclaimed Mr. Raccoon; and forgetting all about his breakfast, he hurried down the path.

Whom should he meet but Mrs. Chipmunk, who was showing off her new parasol made of real butterfly wings. She had just bought it so she was pleased when Mr. Raccoon said, "Your parasol is very pretty, but Mrs. Chipmunk, how can you think of such things! Haven't you heard?"

And before Mrs. Chipmunk could answer, Mr. Raccoon was whispering in her ear, "A beaver boiled a . . . a rat, cut it into several pieces and ate it."

"Oh, no!" cried the chipmunk. "Just wait until I tell my husband," and spinning her parasol, she hurried home. Secretly Mrs. Chipmunk did not like rats at all. The very mention of the name made her nose twitch and caused

her to sneeze. So the only thing to do was not to mention that hateful word, rat.

As she hurried along, thinking about that terrible word, she met Mr. Turtle who was slowly crawling along the woodland path.

"Mr. Turtle, Mr. Turtle," she cried, "how can you be so calm? Don't you know what happened last night?"

"No. What?" answered the turtle, not at all excited at the way in which Mrs. Chipmunk was acting.

"Why, a beaver boiled *two* . . . ugh, chipmunks, cut them into several pieces and ate them!"

Before the turtle could say a word or even act surprised Mrs. Chipmunk hurried home to tell the exciting news. But she found that Mr. Chipmunk was out, and that Mr. Squirrel had come with a bundle of the very freshest nuts.

Mrs. Chipmunk immediately sat down and said, "Oh my, I think I'll faint."

"What happened?" asked the squirrel.

"Why, haven't you heard?" said Mrs. Chipmunk in astonishment. "The beavers boiled three . . . er . . . chipmunks and ate them for dinner."

Mr. Squirrel was horrified, but after a moment, said, "I am indeed deeply grieved, but I still cannot feel as unhappy as if they had eaten a squirrel."

At this, Mrs. Chipmunk was furious, so she quickly added, "That is where you're wrong, Mr. Squirrel. The beavers ate a squirrel for dessert!" Whereupon the squirrel fell over in a dead faint.

When the squirrel was himself again, he asked for a handkerchief, and left Mrs. Chipmunk's home, sobbing as he went. Mr. Chipmunk, who just was coming home, stopped the sobbing squirrel and asked him why he was crying.

"Haven't you heard what terrible danger threatens us?" cried the squirrel. "The beavers have begun eating up all the chipmunks and the squirrels." Then, weeping still more, he

added, "How can anyone eat meat when there are such delicious nuts to be had? I cannot understand it."

Mr. Chipmunk didn't say a word, but walked sadly back to his house.

A few days later when Mr. Chipmunk was entertaining his friends the bear, the deer, and the porcupine for supper, he said, "Have you heard the terrible story about the beaver?" His friends looked at him in surprise, so he went on, "Shall I tell you this terrible thing *before* or *after* we eat?"

The porcupine said, "Let's eat first. I don't want to get excited on an empty stomach."

The deer said, "Let's hear the story while we are eating."

But the big bear said, "Let's hear the story before we sup. Then we can think about it while we eat."

And so the chipmunk told the story. "This summer is a most unhappy one. While we suffer from the heat and stay at home, the beavers secretly sneak out, hunt, kill and boil all the animals they can find." And with that, the chipmunk pushed away his plate and laid his head down on the table and sobbed.

The porcupine was so frightened that he made himself as small as a mouse. "No doubt the beavers are on their way here to boil and eat us, too," he cried. And with that, he pushed away his plate, laid his head down on the table and cried.

The deer shuddered and said, "Perhaps the beavers are hiding in your garden, Mr. Chipmunk." And he, too, pushed away his plate, laid his head down on the table and cried.

But the big bear did not cry. Jumping up he roared, "I'll punish them! I'll eat THEM up! Let's go to the old beaver's lodge and declare war!"

Immediately, the deer, the porcupine, and the chipmunk stopped crying and began to shout: "War! War!"

And so, away they marched — the bear in the lead — to the old beaver's home.

Arriving at the beaver's lodge, the bear
knocked at the door with such fury that the
whole lodge shook. Then, breaking down the
door, they marched into the kitchen where the
beaver family was standing around, looking at
a big pot of water which was boiling on the
stove.

"Aha!" shouted the bear, "just about to boil another animal!" Catching hold of Mr. Beaver with his big left paw, he grabbed hold of Mrs. Beaver and her daughter with his big right paw.

Frightened, the three beavers began to tremble. "What has happened?" cried the old beaver. "What are you doing to us?"

"War! War!" cried the porcupine, as he shook his quills.

"But what have we done?" asked the beaver.

"What a question!" roared the bear. "What a question! No doubt you thought we'd never find out about your nightly hunting trips! No doubt you thought you could go on forever, boiling and eating all the animals."

The beavers were so frightened their hair almost turned white. But Mrs. Beaver finally found the courage to say, "How silly. You know we only eat bark."

But the bear didn't believe her, and growling fiercely, ordered the porcupine and the chipmunk to search the house. Of course they found nothing but bark. The bear, puzzled, suggested, "No doubt you boil the animals at night."

"Nonsense," answered the beaver. "That isn't true. Look around some more. Ask the other animals, my neighbors, and if you find I am not telling the truth, I will boil and eat myself."

The bear agreed to this, and ordering the porcupine to watch the beaver's lodge, he took the chipmunk aside and asked him if the story he had heard about the beavers was true.

After thinking hard, the chipmunk said, "Well, maybe the beavers don't eat all kinds of animals, but they did eat all the chipmunks and squirrels they could get hold of."

"Who told you this?" asked the bear.

"Well, it was Mr. Squirrel, who sells us nuts."

Off went Mr. Bear to see the squirrel. Again he asked if the story he had heard about the beavers was true.

The squirrel thought long and hard, then said, "Well, perhaps the beavers didn't eat all the chipmunks and squirrels, but they did eat three chipmunks and one squirrel."

"Who told you this?" asked the bear.

"Mrs. Chipmunk told me," answered the squirrel.

So the bear went back to the chipmunks'
home to question Mrs. Chipmunk. She thought
a while and then said, "The very thought of
it makes me faint. But — well, Mr. Raccoon
told me that a . . . rat had been thrown into
boiling water and been eaten up by a beaver."

It was quite brave of Mrs. Chipmunk to
say this, for she could not bear to say the
word "rat." Her nose began to twitch and she
sneezed loud and long.

The bear did not wait for her to stop

sneezing, but rushed to find Mr. Raccoon. Mr. Raccoon was very annoyed at being asked questions. The bear looked at him so sternly, however, that after he had thought a while, he said, "Well, if you have to know, Mrs. Rabbit told me that the beaver had a fight with a mouse and had thrown her into hot water and cut her up into several pieces."

"Aha!" said the bear and set out to find Mrs. Rabbit. Again he asked the same question.

"Oh, dear," said Mrs. Rabbit, "I really don't remember, but it seems to me that Mrs. Woodchuck told me a beaver had a fight with a mouse, and threw her into boiling water and ate her."

The bear went to Mrs. Woodchuck's house. She thought and thought and finally said: "Well, it was a mouse. They didn't eat her, but they did boil her."

"And who told you that?" asked the bear.
"The crow that lives in the tree near the
beaver's lodge, of course," she answered.

Off went the bear to visit the crow who was very glad to see him, for no one ever came to see her. She was not quite so happy when the bear said, "I declared war on the beavers, for I have heard that they have begun to eat up all the animals." Coming closer to the crow, he went on, "We are going to kill and eat all the beavers because you have seen, with your own eyes, that the old beaver threw a mouse into boiling water."

The skinny crow was very frightened and cried, "War? You've declared war? Oh dear, I didn't see anything. I heard a splash — maybe I didn't — yes I did — maybe I didn't . . ." and with that she fainted right into the bear's arms. So the bear gave her some water, and went below to the beaver's lodge where he found the little mouse waiting in front of it.

"Let me help!" cried the mouse, who had heard that the beavers were in danger. "They are my friends; they are good neighbors."

"They don't need anyone's help," said the bear as he went inside to apologize to the beaver family.

So now the beavers were all very happy and invited the bear, the porcupine, the deer, the chipmunk, and the little mouse, to stay and visit a while. The little mouse, who was quite excited, jumped up on the table and began to sing:

*The crow, she lied about a mouse.*
*The lie grew bigger than a house,*
*And from this teeny-weeny bubble*
*Came plenty, yes plenty, oh, plenty of*
   *trouble!*

Then the bear, the deer, the porcupine, the
chipmunk and the beavers all joined the mouse
in his song.

And all the animals promised that, from that day on, they would remain fast friends and think twice before repeating a story.